D1069049

# BLACK PANTHER

## A NATION UNDER OUR FEET: PART 1

MARVEL

**ABDOBOOKS.COM**

Reinforced library bound edition published in 2020 by Spotlight, a division of ABDO, PO Box 398166, Minneapolis, Minnesota 55439. Spotlight produces high-quality reinforced library bound editions for schools and libraries. Published by agreement with Marvel Characters, Inc.

Printed in the United States of America, North Mankato, Minnesota.
042019
092019

Library of Congress Control Number: 2018965952

Publisher's Cataloging-in-Publication Data

Names: Coates, Ta-Nehisi, author. | Stelfreeze, Brian; Martin, Laura; Sprouse, Chris; Story, Karl, illustrators.
Title: A nation under our feet / writer: Ta-Nehisi Coates; art: Brian Stelfreeze ; Laura Martin ; Chris Sprouse ; Karl Story.
Description: Minneapolis, Minnesota : Spotlight, 2020 | Series: Black Panther
Summary: With a dramatic upheaval in Wakanda on the horizon, T'Challa knows his kingdom needs to change to survive, but he struggles to find balance in his roles as king and the Black Panther.
Identifiers: ISBN 9781532143519 (pt. 1 ; lib. bdg.) | ISBN 9781532143526 (pt. 2 ; lib. bdg.) | ISBN 9781532143533 (pt. 3 ; lib. bdg.) | ISBN 9781532143540 (pt. 4 ; lib. bdg.) | ISBN 9781532143557 (pt. 5 ; lib. bdg.) | ISBN 9781532143564 (pt. 6 ; lib. bdg.)
Subjects: LCSH: Black Panther (Fictitious character)--Juvenile fiction. | Superheroes--Juvenile fiction. | Kings and rulers--Juvenile fiction. | Graphic novels--Juvenile fiction. | T'Challa, of Wakanda (Fictitious character)--Juvenile fiction.
Classification: DDC 741.5--dc23

**Spotlight**

A Division of ABDO
abdobooks.com

# BLACK PANTHER

is the ancestral ceremonial title of **T'CHALLA**, the king of Wakanda. T'Challa splits his time between protecting his kingdom, with the aid of his elite female royal guard, the **DORA MILAJE**, and helping protect the entire world, as a member of super hero teams such as the Avengers and the Ultimates.

The African nation **WAKANDA** is the most technologically advanced society on the globe. It sits upon a large deposit of an extremely rare natural resource called vibranium. Wakanda long boasted of having never been conquered. But recent events -- a biblical flood that killed thousands, a coup orchestrated by Doctor Doom, an invasion by the villain Thanos -- have humbled the kingdom.

T'Challa recently spent some time away from the throne. His sister **SHURI** had been ruling as both queen and Black Panther in his absence, but she died defending Wakanda against Thanos' army.

Now T'Challa is king once more, but the people of Wakanda are restless...

I AM THE ORPHAN-KING.
WHO DEFIED THE BLOOD...
YOU HAVE NO PEOPLE. YOU ARE NO LONGER MY SON.
WHO DEFIED HIS COUNTRY...
YOU SPENT YOUR LIFE BUILDING A PERFECT KINGDOM, AND NOW YOU HAVE BEEN CAST OUT.
AND WAS DIVIDED FROM YOU.
YOU HAVE LOST YOUR WAY, MY KING.

"YOU HAVE LOST YOUR SOUL."
THE GREAT MOUND

I CAME HERE TO PRAISE THE HEART OF MY COUNTRY, THE VIBRANIUM MINERS OF THE GREAT MOUND. FOR I AM THEIR KING AND I LOVE THEM AS THE FATHER LOVES THE CHILD.

BUT AMONG MY CHILDREN, ALL I FOUND WAS HATE.

THE HATE SPREAD.
BACK, YOU FILTHY DOGS! ON YOUR KNEES BEFORE YOUR KING!

AND SO THERE IS WAR.

THE HATE DID NOT RISE ON ITS OWN.

DECEIVERS ARE LOOSE IN MY KINGDOM.

AND SO THE HATE SPREADS.
DEATH TO TYRANTS!
A THRONE FOR WAKANDANS!

CONSUMING THE BODY OF THE NATION. DIVIDING ME FROM MY VERY BLOOD.

NOW THEY CALL ME *HARAMU-FAL*-- THE ORPHAN-KING.

BUT I HAVE NOT FORGOTTEN MY NAME.

DAMISA-SARKI--THE PANTHER.

MY NAME IS MY NATURE. I CAN TRACK A BODY THROUGH WIND AND RAIN, FOR I TRACK NOT THE BODY, BUT THE SOUL WITHIN.

BUT THE DECEIVER'S SCENT HAS GONE STALE.

MY KING, WE MUST GO!
HER POWER FADES.

CALL THE SOLDIERS BACK, MY KING! WE MUST NOT MASSACRE OUR OWN PEOPLE!

AND I MUST NOW RECKON WITH WHAT IS LOOSE IN MY COUNTRY.

THE HATE FADES.

AND WE MUST NOW RECKON WITH WHAT WE HAVE DONE TO OUR OWN BLOOD.

writer **TA-NEHISI COATES**
artist **BRIAN STELFREEZE**
color artist **LAURA MARTIN**

# A NATIO
# UNDER OUR

letterer **VC's JOE SABINO**
logo **RIAN HUGHES** design **MANNY MEDEROS**
variant covers by **BRIAN STELFREEZE**
**FELIPE SMITH, ALEX ROSS, SKOTTIE YOUNG, OLIVIER COIPEL, SANFORD GREENE, RYAN SOOK, DISNEY INTERACTIVE**
cover by **BRIAN STELFREEZE**
assistant editor **CHRIS ROBINSON**
editor **WIL MOSS**
executive editor **TOM BREVOORT**

editor in chief **AXEL ALONSO** chief creative officer **JOE QUESADA** publisher **DAN BUCKLEY** executive producer **ALAN FINE**

**BLACK PANTHER** created by **STAN LEE & JACK KIRBY**

ON
FEET
part 1

THERE ARE NO ASSASSINS AMONG THE DORA MILAJE, MOTHER. THE DORA MILAJE ARE THE NATION.
THE GOLDEN CITY, CAPITAL OF WAKANDA
OUR FORCES ARE DRAWN FROM ALL THE TRIBES, AND FORGED INTO A SINGULAR EMBLEM OF THE COUNTRY. WE ARE THE BLOOD-ALLOY OF WAKANDA ITSELF.
NONE KNOW THIS MORE THAN ANEKA, OUR CAPTAIN, YOUR PRISONER. SHE WOULD DIE FOR THE FUTURE OF WAKANDA. SHE WOULD DIE FOR OUR KING. SHE WOULD DIE FOR YOU.

BUT WAKANDA IS IN CHAOS, MOTHER. ROADS ARE INFESTED WITH ROBBERS. FARMERS ARE CUT DOWN IN THEIR OWN FIELDS. VILLAINY RULES. JUSTICE IS A SLAVE.

YOUR DAUGHTER, SHURI, OUR QUEEN, HAS VANISHED. OUR RETURNED KING RULES FROM A SHAKY THRONE. THIS HOUSE HAS FALLEN. NO ONE IS COMING TO SAVE US. AND SO WE MUST SAVE OURSELVES.
THE KIMOYO BAND TELLS THE TALE.

"THE CHIEFTAIN'S OUTRAGES UPON THE GIRLS OF HIS VILLAGE WERE KNOWN. YET HIS LECHERY WAS UNOPPOSED.
"ANEKA SPOKE TO HIM AS FATHERS AND BROTHERS SHOULD HAVE SPOKEN LONG BEFORE.
"AND WHEN SHE WAS NOT HEEDED, SHE DID AS THE HONOR OF WAKANDAN FATHERS AND BROTHERS HAS ALWAYS DEMANDED."

ANEKA STOOD AGAINST THE JACKALS WHO LAY IN WAIT. AND FOR THIS SHE IS BRANDED A MURDERER WHO MUST GIVE HER LIFE.

SPARE HER, MOTHER. SPARE HER THE BASTARD SANCTION OF MEN WHOSE HONOR IS OSTENTATION, WHOSE JUSTICE IS DECEIT.

NO.
YOU ARE DORA MILAJE, CHAMPION OF OUR NATION, CELEBRATED IN FABLES AND SONGS.
BUT NOW YOU STAND BEFORE ME--SHIELD-MAIDEN IN PEASANT'S CLOTHES--PLEADING FOR SOME OTHER STANDARD.
YOU HAVE SAID IT YOURSELF: VILLAINY OVERWHELMS US. AND YOUR ANSWER TO THIS VILLAINY IS TO TURN THE UPHOLDERS OF WAKANDAN LAW INTO ITS FLOUTERS.
NO. YOU ARE EXEMPLARS OF OUR NATION. AND IF YOU WILL NOT SERVE IN LIFE, YOU WILL SERVE IN DEATH.
I TAKE NO JOY IN DOING MY DUTY. BUT I WILL DO IT, EVEN AS OTHERS FALTER.

FOR THE LIFE OF HER SON, MY MOTHER GAVE UP HER OWN.
FOR THE LIFE OF HIS NATION, MY FATHER DID THE SAME.
RAMONDA, MY FATHER'S SECOND WIFE AND WIDOW, IS AS MUCH MY MOTHER AS THE MOTHER WHO DIED FOR ME.
WHAT HAPPENED, MY SON?
I APPEALED TO THEM TO RETURN TO WORK--THAT IN THESE TIMES WE NEEDED THEM MORE THAN EVER.

AND DID THEY HEAR YOU?

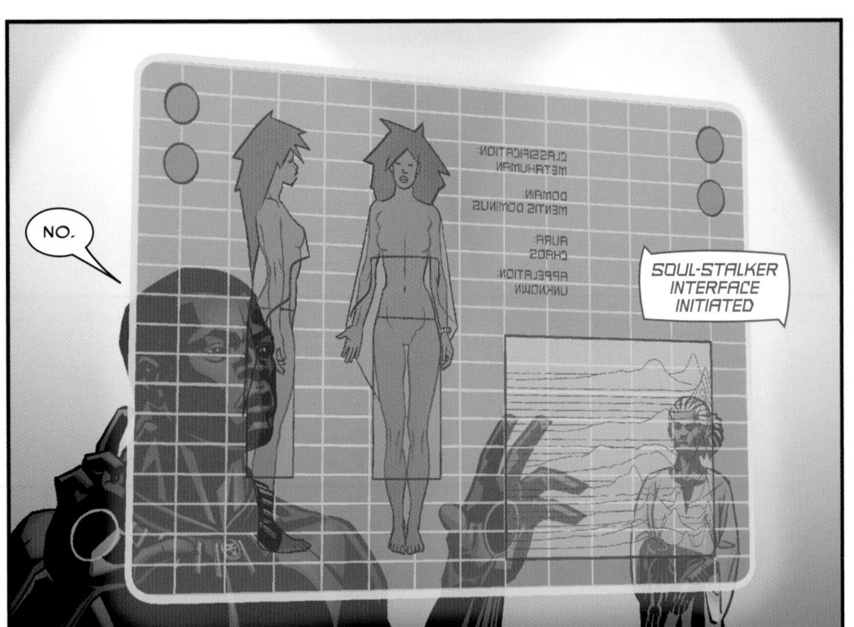
NO.
SOUL-STALKER INTERFACE INITIATED

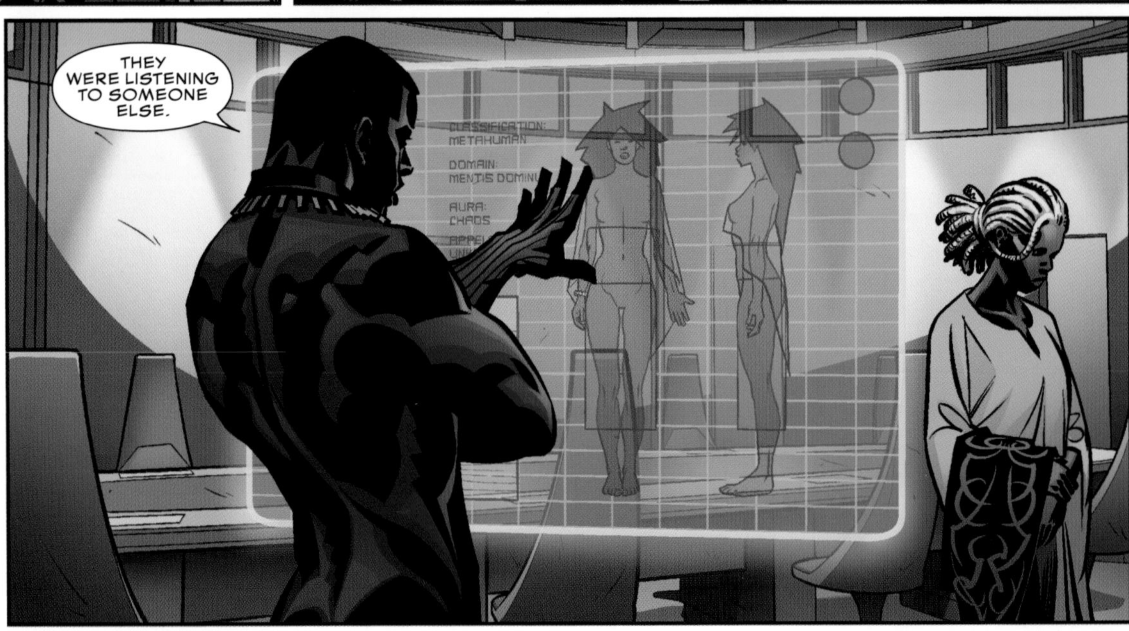
THEY WERE LISTENING TO SOMEONE ELSE.
CLASSIFICATION:
METAHUMAN
DOMAIN:
AURA:
CHAOS

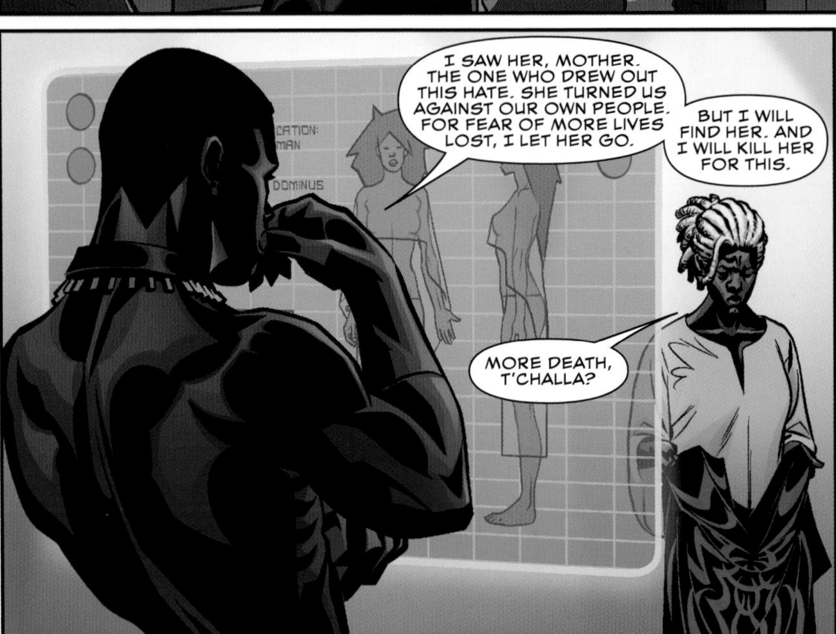
I SAW HER, MOTHER. THE ONE WHO DREW OUT THIS HATE. SHE TURNED US AGAINST OUR OWN PEOPLE. FOR FEAR OF MORE LIVES LOST, I LET HER GO.
BUT I WILL FIND HER. AND I WILL KILL HER FOR THIS.
MORE DEATH, T'CHALLA?

TODAY I UPHELD AN EXECUTION FOR ONE OF OUR OWN ADORED ONES. IT WAS MY DUTY, AND I WOULD DO IT AGAIN. BUT I AM NOT BLIND TO WHAT THIS MEANS.

WAKANDA IS IN STRIFE-- INVASION, FLOOD, INFILTRATION...

REGICIDE.

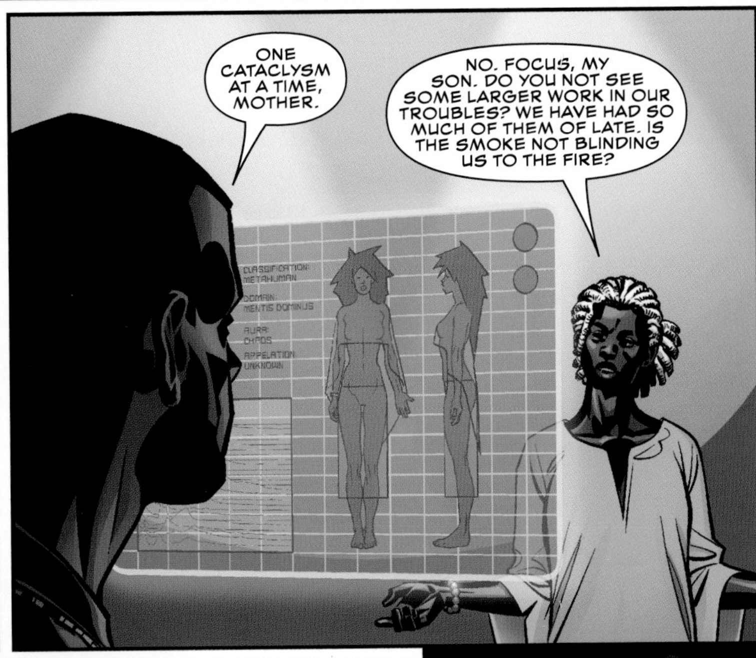
ONE CATACLYSM AT A TIME, MOTHER.
NO. FOCUS, MY SON. DO YOU NOT SEE SOME LARGER WORK IN OUR TROUBLES? WE HAVE HAD SO MUCH OF THEM OF LATE. IS THE SMOKE NOT BLINDING US TO THE FIRE?
CLASSIFICATION: METAHUMAN
DOMAIN: MENTIS DOMINUS
AURA: CHAOS
APPELATION: UNKNOWN

I SAW THE FIRE RIGHT THERE, IN HER EYES, RIGHT WHEN SHE TURNED INNOCENT MEN AGAINST THEIR COUNTRY.

THEN DO WHAT YOU MUST, T'CHALLA. BUT DON'T LOSE YOURSELF. YOU ARE NOT A SOLDIER. YOU ARE A KING.

AND IT IS NOT ENOUGH TO BE THE SWORD, YOU MUST BE THE INTELLIGENCE BEHIND IT.

MEANWHILE...
"I SAW AN AGONY IN THEM SO COMPLETE THAT IT ECLIPSED EVERYTHING...

"DUTY TO COUNTRY, KING, EVEN EACH OTHER. AGONY OVER ALL.

"HUMILIATION, SADNESS, ALL AGONY. AND THEN UNDER THE AGONY, I SAW SOMETHING ELSE..."

RAGE.

AND YOU ENCOURAGED THAT RAGE?
NO. I REVEALED TO THEM, IN ALL THEIR AGONY, THEIR DEEPER, TRUER SELVES.
I GAVE THEM A GIFT. I ENCOURAGED NOTHING, FOR I COME TO WAKANDA NOT AS AN EXHORTER, BUT AS A *LIBERATOR.*
DO THEY STILL FEAR *HARAMU-FAL?*
THEY HAVE LEARNED THAT THERE ARE GREATER AGONIES THAN THE WRATH OF KINGS.
DO THE PEOPLE NOW HATE HIM?
HAVEN'T YOU BEEN LISTENING? THE GOLDEN CITY WAS BREACHED. THEIR CHILDREN WERE DROWNED AND BURNED AND *HARAMU-FAL* COULD NOT SHIELD THEM.
THE PEOPLE DON'T *HATE* THEIR KING, TETU. THEY ARE *ASHAMED* OF HIM.

HAVE THE AURAS PASSED?
THE AURAS NEVER TRULY PASS. THE AGONY WAS IN ME. I FELT IT ALL.

IT WAS THE AGONY OF LABOR, ZENZI. IT HAD TO BE DONE. IT WAS THE AGONY OF BIRTHING OUR NEW NATION.

FOR OUT OF THE RAGE SHALL COME ANOTHER WAKANDA.

THE NIGANDAN BORDER REGION
AND A BETTER AND BRIGHTER WORLD.

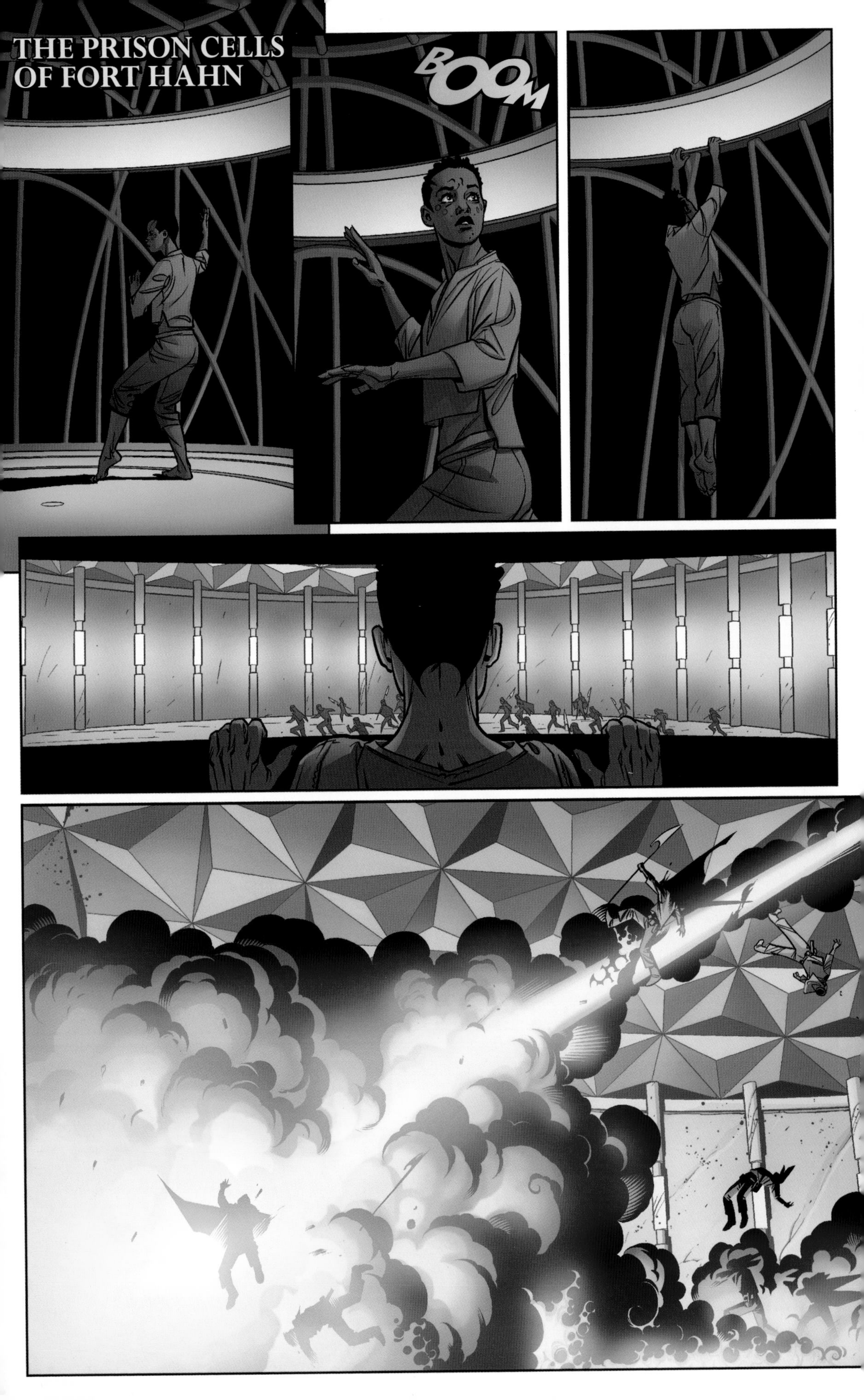
THE PRISON CELLS OF FORT HAHN
BOOM

BACK AWAY FROM THE WALL, ANEKA.
AYO? NO. DON'T DO IT.
BACK AWAY!

AYO, DON'T DO THIS. NOT FOR ME.

DON'T THROW IT AWAY, BELOVED.

GET DOW-- NNNH!

I KNEW IT WAS YOU. IT COULD HAVE ONLY BEEN YOU.
I TRIED THEIR WAY, BELOVED.

I KNOW. AND NOW THEY ARE GOING TO KILL US BOTH.
THEY WERE GOING TO KILL US BOTH ANYWAY. WHEN THEY CONDEMNED YOU, DEAR HEART, THEY CONDEMNED ME.

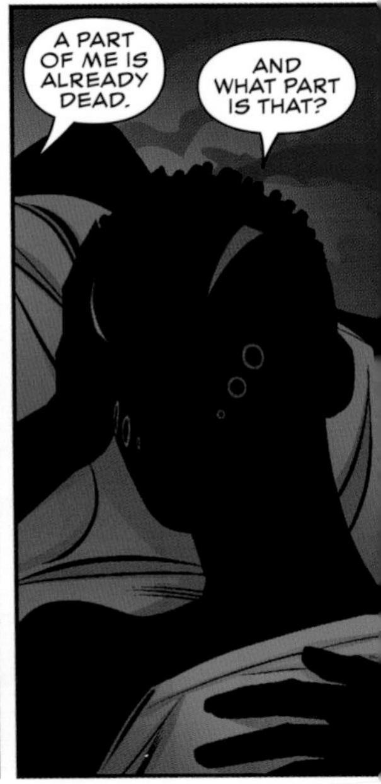
A PART OF ME IS ALREADY DEAD.
AND WHAT PART IS THAT?

THE PART OF ME THAT WAS *DORA MILAJE.* THE PART OF ME THAT ONCE LIVED FOR OUR KING.

WAKANDA IS FALLING, BELOVED. NOT EVEN *DAMISA-SARKI* CAN SAVE US.
DOES HE EVEN CARE, ANEKA? DID HE ***EVER*** CARE?
DOES IT EVEN MATTER? HAS IT EVER MATTERED?

AYO, THEY ARE GOING TO KILL US, SO I SHALL SPEAK AS MY DEAD SELF, WHICH IS MY BEST SELF. I AM TIRED OF LIVING AND DYING ON THE BLOOD-RIGHT OF ONE MAN.
NO ONE MAN SHOULD HAVE THAT MUCH POWER.

I KNEW IT WAS YOU, BELOVED. ONLY YOU WOULD BE SO MAD AS TO STEAL THE ***MIDNIGHT ANGEL*** PROTOTYPE.
***BOTH*** PROTOTYPES.
YES...BOTH PROTOTYPES... WELL THEN...

...LET US ACT AS DEAD WOMEN SHOULD.

NECROPOLIS, THE CITY OF THE DEAD
BURIAL SITE OF PREVIOUS BLACK PANTHERS
HOW LONG MUST I BE DIVIDED FROM MY OWN PEOPLE?

FROM MY COUNTRY...

FROM MY OWN BLOOD?

RESUSCITATION FAILURE
SHURI...

...SISTER...
...HOW LONG MUST I BE PARTED FROM YOU?
RESUSCITATION FAILURE
TO BE CONTINUED

# BLACK PANTHER

## COLLECT THEM ALL!

**Set of 6 Hardcover Books ISBN: 978-1-5321-4350-2**

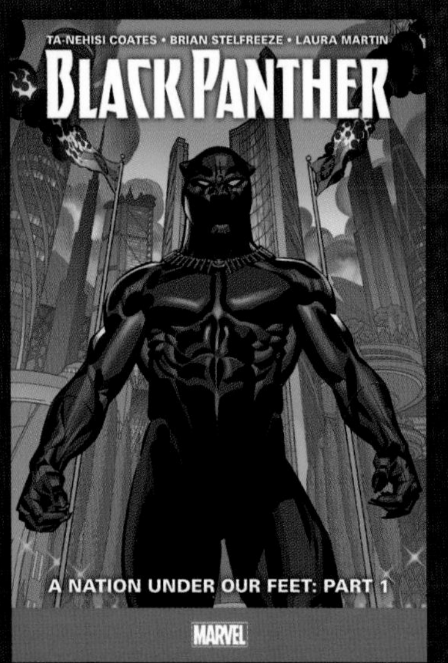


**Hardcover Book ISBN 978-1-5321-4351-9**

**Hardcover Book ISBN 978-1-5321-4352-6**

**Hardcover Book ISBN 978-1-5321-4353-3**

**Hardcover Book ISBN 978-1-5321-4354-0**

**Hardcover Book ISBN 978-1-5321-4355-7**

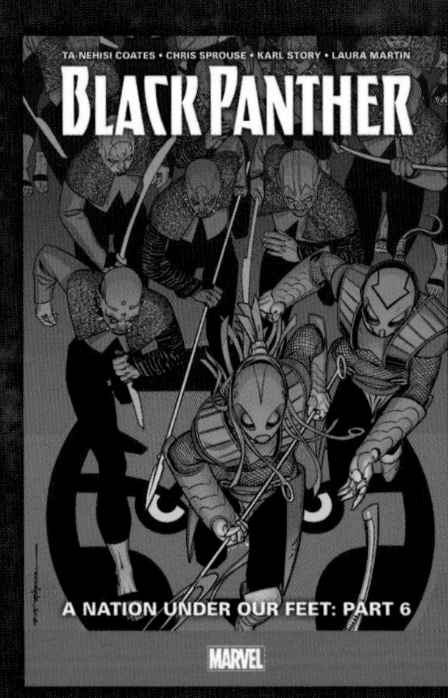


**Hardcover Book ISBN 978-1-5321-4356-4**